Introduction

Pinkie Pie was visiting the Crystal Empire Castle with a special purpose. She bounced into the nursery. "Baby Flurry Heart!" she exclaimed, "I realized the other day that you get to experience everything in Equestria for the first time ever!"

That made Pinkie super happy.

Then she realized there were so many things that happened before Flurry Heart was born, and the royal baby would never get to experience them, and that made Pinkie sad.

But then Pinkie Pie had the **BEST IDEA EVER.** "I'm going to make you a book about all the amazing things you missed and all the amazing things you get to look forward to!" Pinkie continued, "I call it . . ."

This book belongs to:
Baby Flurry Heart

From:

Pinkie Pie

My Little Pony

5- Minute Stories

My Little Pony: 5-Minute Stories
HASBRO and its logo, MY LITTLE PONY and all related characters are trademarks of Hasbro
and are used with permission. © 2021 Hasbro. All Rights Reserved. Manufactured in Italy.

Library of Congress Control Number: 2020943255
ISBN 978-0-06-303764-9

21 22 23 24   RTLO   10 9 8 7 6 5 4 3 2

❖

Originally published by Little, Brown and Company in 2017.

Licensed by:

My Little Pony

5- Minute Stories

By Pinkie Pie
Adapted by Magnolia Belle

HARPER
*An Imprint of HarperCollins*Publishers

STORIES!

THE ROYAL WEDDING

When two ponies **FALL IN LOVE,** they get married and have a **WEDDING.**

It's a GINORMOUS party with rings and dancing and a GREAT BIG CAKE with two ponies on top. Not real ponies. They're little toy ponies.

When Princess Cadance and Shining Armor got married, it was one of the BIGGEST weddings Canterlot had ever seen.

Ponies came from all over Equestria and everypony was

SUPER EXCITED!

Well, not EVERYpony.

PRINCESS TWILIGHT SPARKLE was not excited at all. Shining Armor was her big brother, and she was **UPSET** because she didn't even know that he was planning to get married. When she read the invitation, she couldn't believe her eyes.

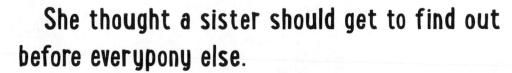

She thought a sister should get to find out before everypony else.

Twilight's sadness about the wedding didn't last long. As she kept reading the invitation, she quickly realized that her brother was going to marry Princess Cadance! Twilight Sparkle completely changed her mind and **FLIPPED OUT WITH EXCITEMENT.**

Twilight Sparkle loved Princess Cadance. She had known her all her life and already felt like she was family. Princess Cadance used to foal-sit Twilight when she was very young. Twilight could not wait to have Princess Cadance as her new **BIG SISTER.**

Since Princess Twilight Sparkle LOVED Shining Armor and Princess Cadance so much, she wanted their wedding to be SPECTACULAR. She gathered all her closest friends, including Fluttershy, Pinkie Pie, Applejack, Rainbow Dash, and Rarity, and asked for their help to make it the

BEST WEDDING EVER.

They all packed up and took the FRIENDSHIP EXPRESS to Canterlot. As the train drew closer to Canterlot, the ponies couldn't contain their excitement. Everypony was buzzing knowing that, soon, Princess Cadance and Shining Armor would be married! And Twilight was going to have a new sister! It was going to be perfect. What could go wrong?

On the big day of the wedding, chaos erupted when the ponies discovered that Princess Cadance wasn't really Princess Cadance. She was CHRYSALIS, queen of the Changelings, IN DISGUISE!

Chrysalis was planning on ruling the Kingdom disguised as Princess Cadance. But being discovered didn't ruin her plans.

Not even the brave Shining Armor could stop the evil villain. Chrysalis put a **SPELL** on Shining Armor. She was going to soak up his love and use it as power to rule over all Equestria.

With her scary Changelings by her side, she would be

UNSTOPPABLE.

Twilight Sparkle and the other ponies TRIED TO STOP Chrysalis. She blasted the Changelings with the magic from her horn, dodging the scary creatures as they led their attack.

But for every Changeling Twilight Sparkle BLASTED, two more popped up in its place. The Changelings were just too strong, and there were too many of them.

The ponies knew Chrysalis controlled the Changelings. If they had any chance of getting rid of the Changelings, they were going to need to defeat Chrysalis. But how?

The ponies needed something EVEN STRONGER than their powers to take down the villain.

After finally finding the real Princess Cadance, Pinkie Pie had a brilliant idea! What if they could channel Shining Armor and Princess Cadance's **TRUE LOVE?!** The couple was willing to try anything to save their Kingdom from Chrysalis's evil plans. Focusing all their love, Shining Armor and Princess Cadance touched horns. The power of their love echoed through the Kingdom, breaking Chrysalis's spell.

KA-POW

The **SHOCK WAVE OF LOVE** was so **POWERFUL**, it **BLASTED** Chrysalis and all her Changelings back to the Changeling Kingdom.

With Chrysalis gone, Shining Armor and Princess Cadance were finally able to have their wedding.

And there were rings and dancing and a
GREAT BIG CAKE
with two little ponies on top.

Plus, Twilight Sparkle finally had her new sister! Everypony in the Kingdom was happy for the new royal couple and was safe once again. And it was all thanks to Twilight and her friends.

BEST. WEDDING. EVER!

FOAL-SITTING 101

Moms and dads are pretty busy ponies, and they aren't always able to spend every minute of every day with their foals. Did you know that *foal* is another word for baby pony? It's true.

It's also true that there are places the pony parents have to go, like jobs and fancy dinners with other moms and dads.

That's where FOAL-SITTERS come in.

Foal-sitters are **NOT** ponies who sit on little foals.

HA-HA!

If that's all foal-sitters had to do, that would be a pretty easy job. Nope, foal-sitters have much more responsibility than just sitting around all day!

Foal-sitters make sure little colts and fillies have everything they need while their parents are away. After all, foals can't take care of themselves. In Equestria, little boy and girl ponies are called *colts* and *fillies*. Foal-sitters help them feel safe and warm, and sometimes they even help them . . .

HAVE FUN.

Foal-sitting is no trot in the park. Well, sometimes they trot in the park. In order to get some fresh air for the little colts and fillies, foal-sitters will put them in a stroller or even a baby horse carriage.

Foal-sitters take them to the park to explore all the cool things outside. Like the trees, hills, birds, or even a grumpy old pony eating popcorn! There are so many things to see and do at the park.

Did you know that Pinkie Pie is an expert foal-sitter? She knows foal-sitting is intense, and that **STRETCHING** and **WARMING UP** beforehoof is important. Oh, and the perfect pump-up music is a must!

Foal-sitters have to be on their games and ready.
As soon as Mom and Dad leave, anything can happen . . .

LIKE CRYING.

But it's nothing that Pinkie Pie can't handle. Sometimes when foals get upset, it means they're hungry. Foal-sitters are in charge of making sure the foals get healthy, well-rounded meals. But be careful.

Feeding time can get

MESSY!

And sometimes during feeding time, there is

CRYING.

After feeding, bath time is a must. It's fun with all the **BUBBLES** and bath toys. Foal-sitters must use a lot of soap and water to get the foals squeaky clean. It's also important to be quick on your hooves—bath time can get splashy.

But sometimes during bath time, there is

CRYING.

But don't worry! Foal-sitting is not *all* crying. There are also

DIRTY DIAPERS.

But the poor foals can't help it. They are just little baby ponies! Foal-sitters must not be afraid of dirty diapers. Just a pinched nose, some wipes, and lots of baby powder will do the trick!

And then it is time for bed. Little fillies and colts need to be tucked in so sweetly. A good

BEDTIME STORY

also doesn't hurt when putting them to rest. Once the foals are snoozing away, a foal-sitter must quietly tip-toe out of the room. Oh, and be sure to whisper. Remember: never wake a sleeping foal!

Being a foal-sitter is never boring! Did you know baby ponies can start flying and using **MAGIC** very early on? They

can get into all sorts of things, and foal-sitters have to really keep an eye on them. All they want to do is play!

Pinkie Pie was right. All that stretching, warming up, and pump-up music was totally worth it. She is able to catch the little foals when they fly away. PHEW!

Foal-sitting is definitely a lot of work. Little foals might be a hoof-ful sometimes and can wear a pony out. And sometimes it will be so tiring that even a foal-sitter will CRY! When this happens, just remember that everything will be okay. Mom and Dad will be home soon.

YOU CAN DO THIS!

Pinkie Pie did it! Everypony was in bed by the time the pony parents got home. Great job, Pinkie! At the end of the day, when a foal-sitter knows she has made a good impression, it makes it . . .

ALL WORTH IT.

Ponies in Equestria come in all **SHAPES, COLORS, AND SIZES.** The kinds of ponies they are determine how they shape the world around them.

There are **EARTH PONIES,** who get their **STRENGTH FROM THE LAND.**

Earth ponies have a special **CONNECTION TO NATURE.** They love plants and animals. It's no problem for these Earth ponies to pull heavy plows and load large bales of hay onto the carts.

Earth ponies, like the Apple family, can grow food. Although they can't fly like Pegasi or cast spells like Unicorns, their special connection to the Earth makes them very important in Equestria. There is nothing more MAGICAL than the STRENGTH of the good, true heart of an Earth pony.

There are the WINGED PEGASI, who soar through the skies and CONTROL THE WEATHER. This comes in handy when the Earth ponies need to water their crops! Pegasi can create thunderstorms. But these ponies need to be careful. Getting struck by lightning can be pretty shocking!

Their wings allow them to fly in the sky and walk on clouds. Well, sometimes they walk, and then sometimes they speed, like Rainbow Dash! She can go fast enough to create a sonic rainboom. Pegasi like to feel the wind beneath their wings and FLY FREE.

There are **UNICORNS,** who can use their horns to perform **GREAT MAGIC.**

With their magic, they can LEVITATE and make THINGS APPEAR from nowhere. Sometimes they even use MAGIC FOR PRANKS. They just concentrate their powers in their horn, and POOF! They can cast magic spells. But not everypony thinks the prank is funny. Especially when you're the one stuck with a very silly mustache!

Then there is a very special kind of pony called an ALICORN. Alicorns have cute HORNS and adorable WINGS. Very few ponies have both. That makes

ALICORNS SUPER RARE.

Flurry Heart, the daughter of Shining Armor and Princess Cadance, is the littlest— and cutest!—Alicorn in Equestria.

Other known **ALICORNS** in Equestria are Flurry Heart's mom Princess Cadance, Princess Celestia, Princess Twilight Sparkle, and Princess Luna.

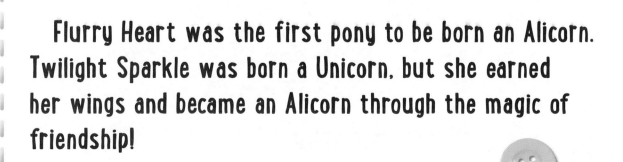

Flurry Heart was the first pony to be born an Alicorn. Twilight Sparkle was born a Unicorn, but she earned her wings and became an Alicorn through the magic of friendship!

Alicorns have elements of all different kinds of ponies. They use **MAGIC** like Unicorns. By concentrating her magic in her horn, Twilight Sparkle can cast powerful spells. And, well, sometimes Pinkie Pie likes to help.

They **FLY** through the sky like Pegasi. And they can get **POWER FROM THE LAND** like Earth ponies. That makes them

SUPER SPECIAL.

Being an Alicorn also means that they have a

HUGE RESPONSIBILITY.

Alicorns are DESTINED for

BIG THINGS.

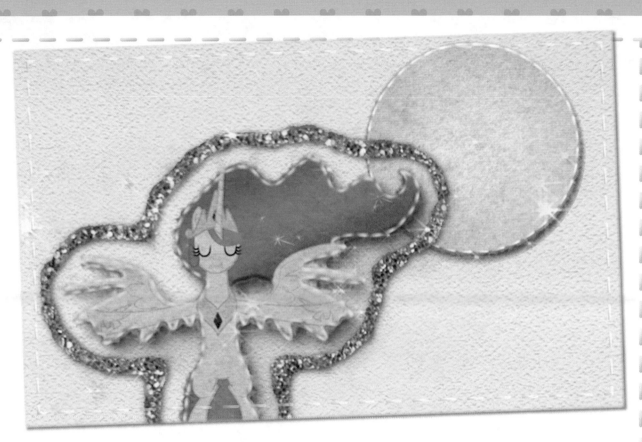

Princess Celestia and Princess Luna are responsible for **RAISING THE SUN AND THE MOON** every single day. That is no small feat!

Princess Cadance rules the Crystal Empire and uses her magic to spread **LOVE** across the land. She **SHARES KINDNESS** and **GOODWILL** everywhere she goes.

Princess Twilight uses the

ELEMENTS OF HARMONY

and the **MAGIC OF FRIENDSHIP**
to protect all Equestria. She gets a little help
from her awesome friends, of course.

That means that one day baby Flurry Heart is going to do something PRETTY AMAZING, too.

Nopony knows how yet, but one day,
BABY FLURRY HEART is going to

CHANGE THE WORLD.

CUTIE MARK MAGIC

As ponies grow up, one of the most amazing things that happens to them is getting their CUTIE MARK. It's a wonderful and magical experience that everypony goes through. Come on, Pinkie Pie will show you!

A cutie mark is a special mark on a pony's flank that shows the world who they are and what they love doing. All ponies are **BORN WITHOUT CUTIE MARKS.** Cutie marks magically appear when ponies discover what makes them unique.

Applejack, for instance, has three apples on her flank. That's because she has the best apple orchards in Equestria! That's what makes her special.

Pinkie Pie's cutie mark is a set of three **BALLOONS**. That's because she **LOVES PARTIES** and making **OTHER PONIES HAPPY!**

The anticipation a pony feels before getting a cutie mark can drive some ponies crazy. Sometimes they have **LOTS OF QUESTIONS** about it.

Some ponies get their CUTIE MARKS EARLY, when they are VERY YOUNG.

Others can get them much later.

It can be **SUPER STRESSFUL** for a pony to not know what his or her cutie mark is going to be. Some ponies try anything and everything to **FIGURE IT OUT.**

Some ponies get their cutie marks at the exact same time because they are all connected to one another! Did you know that's how it happened for the CUTIE MARK CRUSADERS?

When they got their cutie marks, they discovered that what sets them apart from other ponies is also what BRINGS THEM TOGETHER.

There's no forcing it. **CUTIE MARKS JUST HAPPEN** when they happen. It's very natural. A pony just needs to trust that they will get their cutie mark eventually.

When cutie marks do happen, they always turn out perfectly. And all the fear and stress ponies may have felt just fade away.

But cutie mark magic doesn't stop there! Ponies have to be careful! They could get a bad case of

CUTIE POX.

That's when ponies break out in **RANDOM CUTIE MARKS** and perform tasks or talents associated with those cutie marks. For instance, when Apple Bloom got a bad case of the cutie pox, she was spinning plates on her head, lifting weights, and she couldn't stop tap-dancing! It was a cutie mark nightmare!

Other strange magic can make a pony's cutie mark switch with another pony's cutie mark.

This happened to the Mane 6 when Twilight Sparkle accidentally cast an unfinished spell. When their cutie marks were switched, the friends didn't know what to do! It was up to Twilight Sparkle to remind her friends of their destinies and save the day!

GOOD FRIENDS CAN HELP a pony get back to normal.

There are even ponies out there who might try to **STEAL CUTIE MARKS** and replace them with something else entirely. Like Starlight Glimmer, who stole everypony's cutie

mark and replaced it with an equal sign so that everypony would be the same! But the Mane 6 were able to restore every cutie mark and save Equestria. So many things can happen with cutie marks!

When it comes to figuring out cutie marks, ponies should just go out and be the best ponies they can be. If they do what they

LOVE

and follow their

HEARTS,

magic will do the rest.

Cutie marks are meant to show the world just how unique and special ponies are. Whether a pony is an amazing apple farmer like Applejack or loves parties like Pinkie Pie, they all have one thing in common: everypony is unique!

THAT'S THE BEST THING ABOUT CUTIE MARKS!

Today, the Crystal Empire is a beautiful paradise, but it wasn't always so nice. For a long time, the Crystal Empire was under an **EVIL** ENCHANTMENT.

A **SUPER BAD PONY** named **KING SOMBRA** put a spell over the entire kingdom. King Sombra's heart was black as night. He did not believe in love or friendship, and he tried to get rid of it. His spell turned the Crystal Empire into a nightmare world!

He even **ENSLAVED** all the Crystal ponies.

He cursed the Crystal Empire and made it **DISAPPEAR FOR ONE THOUSAND YEARS!** When it finally came back, King Sombra came back with it.

Princess Celestia and Princess Luna wanted to
DEFEAT KING SOMBRA. But they knew they
needed somepony special to help the Crystal Empire.

Princess Celestia and Princess Luna summoned Princess Cadance and Shining Armor to the Crystal Empire to **PROTECT IT FROM DARKNESS** and save the Crystal ponies.

Princess Cadance used her magic to spread love and light in order to protect the Crystal Empire. And Shining Armor cast a protection spell. But King Sombra countered Shining Armor's spell, covering Shining Armor's horn in dark crystals that prevented him from using his magic.

Protecting the Crystal Empire was exhausting and drained Princess Cadance of all her strength. So Princess Twilight and her best friends came to

HELP!

Twilight Sparkle, Applejack, Fluttershy, Pinkie Pie, Rarity, and Rainbow Dash **ALL WORKED TOGETHER** and figured out that they needed to find the Crystal Heart

TO SAVE THE EMPIRE.

They could use its magic to focus all the LOVE AND LIGHT the Crystal ponies had inside them. Even though the Crystal ponies were enslaved by King Sombra, the Mane 6 knew that nopony could ever lose the love and light that lives in their hearts.

LOVE

LIGHT

While Princess Cadance and Shining Armor kept protecting everypony, Twilight searched for the

CRYSTAL HEART.

She and Spike **LOOKED HIGH AND LOW.**
Twilight Sparkle then found a hidden staircase.
As they traveled deeper and deeper down the
stairs, they found a mysterious door. It was a
doorway that King Sombra had created with his
dark magic!

Meanwhile, Pinkie Pie and the other ponies threw an awesome Crystal Faire as a distraction. Crystal Faire is a giant celebration and the Crystal Empire's most important tradition. The Faire is a party that strengthens the spirit of love and unity in the Empire. It helps the Crystal ponies protect their Kingdom. They had a flügelhorn and crystal games—it was so much fun!. Everypony loved it. **EVERYPONY EXCEPT KING SOMBRA.**

Twilight and Spike finally FOUND THE CRYSTAL HEART, but King Sombra trapped Twilight. SHE QUICKLY TOSSED THE HEART TO SPIKE.

He ran all the way out to the courtyard to get away with it, but he tripped and DROPPED THE HEART! Everypony's heart jumped as they watched the Crystal Heart tumble toward the ground. But King Sombra was ready—he came out of nowhere and lunged for the precious heart! It seemed like all was lost.

But Shining Armor and Princess Cadance had **NOT LOST HOPE.** Shining Armor picked up Princess Cadance, aimed her like a javelin, **AND THREW HER INTO THE AIR!**

Princess Cadance spread her wings and saved Spike, catching the heart right at the last minute! The Crystal Heart glowed and filled the empire with the power of every single Crystal ponies' love and light. Peace in the Crystal Empire was restored, and

KING SOMBRA WAS DEFEATED!

 The Crystal Empire returned to the enchanted kingdom of love and light that it once was, and all **THE CRYSTAL PONIES CHEERED.**

That is the story of how Princess Cadance and Shining Armor ended up ruling the Crystal Empire, and that is why baby Flurry Heart has the BRAVEST AND MOST AMAZING PARENTS EVER!

HEARTH'S WARMING EVE

Every day in Equestria is special. Some days are special for a specific reason. **THOSE ARE CALLED HOLIDAYS!** There are all kinds of holidays. One of the ponies' favorites is **HEARTH'S WARMING EVE.**

The ponies love riding the train to Canterlot during this season. They watch through the window as sparkly snowflakes fall from the sky. It is the best time of the year!

89

Hearth's Warming Eve is a day when ponies buy presents for other ponies, share delicious sweet things to eat, sing songs, and it's just **THE BEST.**

Pinkie Pie LOVES Hearth's Warming Eve. Her favorite thing about this amazing holiday is the joy of being together with her friends . . . and OH YEAH, the candy is awesome, too! Gingerbread houses and sweet cupcakes are always around to munch on. And don't even get her started on the presents. Pinkie Pie loves presents!

But did you know that Hearth's Warming Eve isn't just about sweets and presents? It actually celebrates something pretty serious. A long time ago, Unicorns, Pegasi, and Earth ponies did not get along.

Back then, Earth ponies grew the food, Pegasi controlled the weather, and Unicorns rose the sun and the moon. The ponies could have worked together in order to live harmoniously.

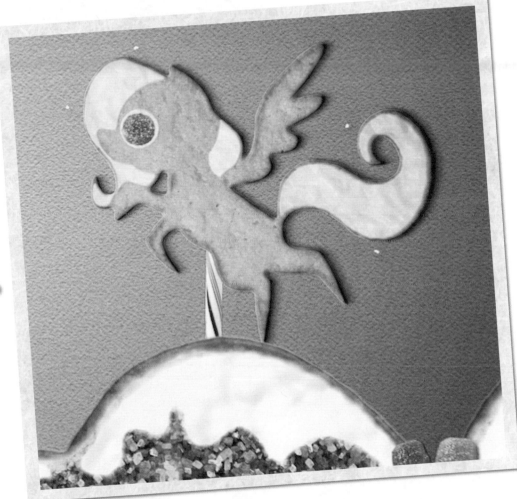

But then the Pegasi and Unicorns thought that they deserved food in payment for the jobs they were doing every day. The problem was, there wasn't enough food to go around. And the ponies began to fight.

The more the ponies fought,

THE WORSE THE WEATHER GOT.

A giant blizzard covered the land in a thick blanket of ice and snow.

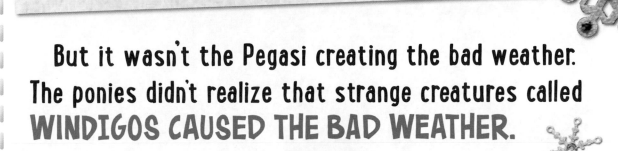

But it wasn't the Pegasi creating the bad weather. The ponies didn't realize that strange creatures called **WINDIGOS CAUSED THE BAD WEATHER.**

WINDIGOS ARE SCARY WIND MONSTERS who feed off anger and turn it into cold and snow. They had been watching the ponies fight, and they knew it was their chance to absorb all the anger and freeze the land.

With all the fighting going on among ponies, the

**WINDIGOS ALMOST FROZE
EVERYPONY FOR GOOD!**

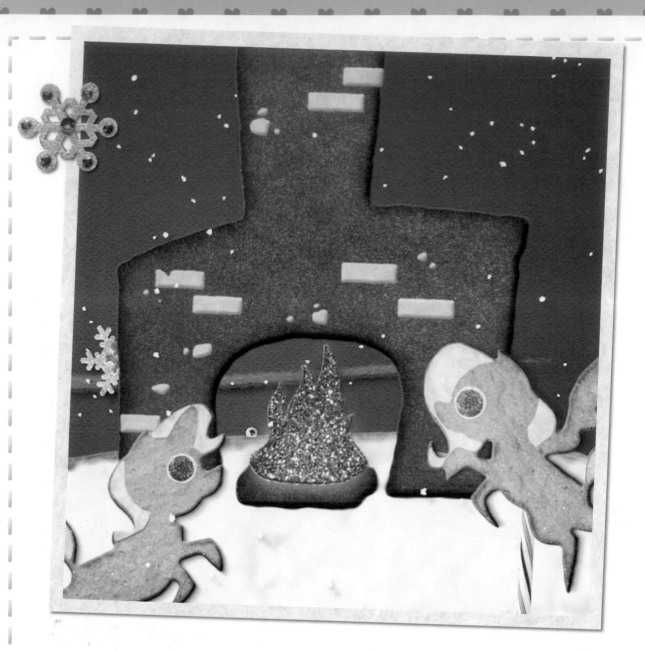

The Earth ponies, Unicorns, and Pegasi found a small cave. It was the only shelter from the blizzard they could find. It felt like all hope was lost. But then they discovered a hearth in the cave. *Hearth* is another word for fireplace or a place where ponies light their fires to stay warm. The ponies huddled around the **TINY HEARTH.**

They started to
SING SONGS AND TELL STORIES.

As they warmed their hooves and their hearts,
the Earth ponies, Pegasi, and Unicorns realized they
WEREN'T THAT DIFFERENT
FROM ONE ANOTHER.

The newfound warmth in their hearts ignited **THE FIRE OF FRIENDSHIP.** The magical fire melted the ice and snow. The grass grew and the flowers bloomed. The land was back to normal!

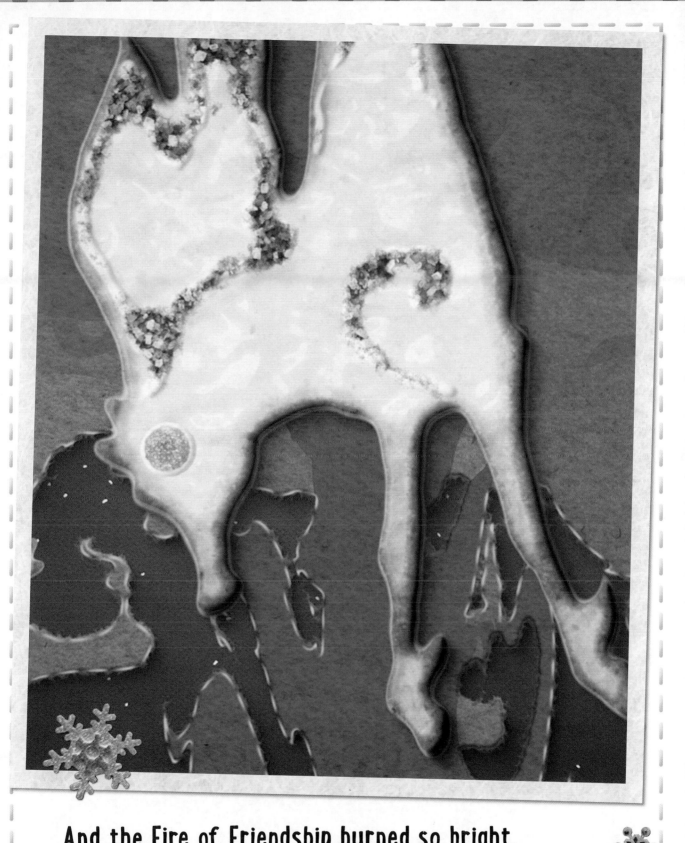

And the Fire of Friendship burned so bright,
it drove back those mean old **WINDIGOS.**

After igniting the Fire of Friendship and restoring peace to their land, the Earth Ponies, Pegasi, and Unicorns came together once again. They agreed that fighting was no way to solve their problems.

They learned to work together. They all decided to live together in harmony, and they named the land

EQUESTRIA!

That's where all the ponies live today! And that is why ponies all sing songs, share food, and give presents on Hearth's Warming Eve. Though the best celebrations happen in Canterlot, of course. Trays of sweets are on every table. Carts stacked high full of presents for everypony can be seen rolling down the streets. It's a truly magical time!

They're **CELEBRATING** the magic of their **FRIENDSHIP** that keeps them all feeling warm, loved, and safe. Happy Hearth's Warming Eve, everyone!

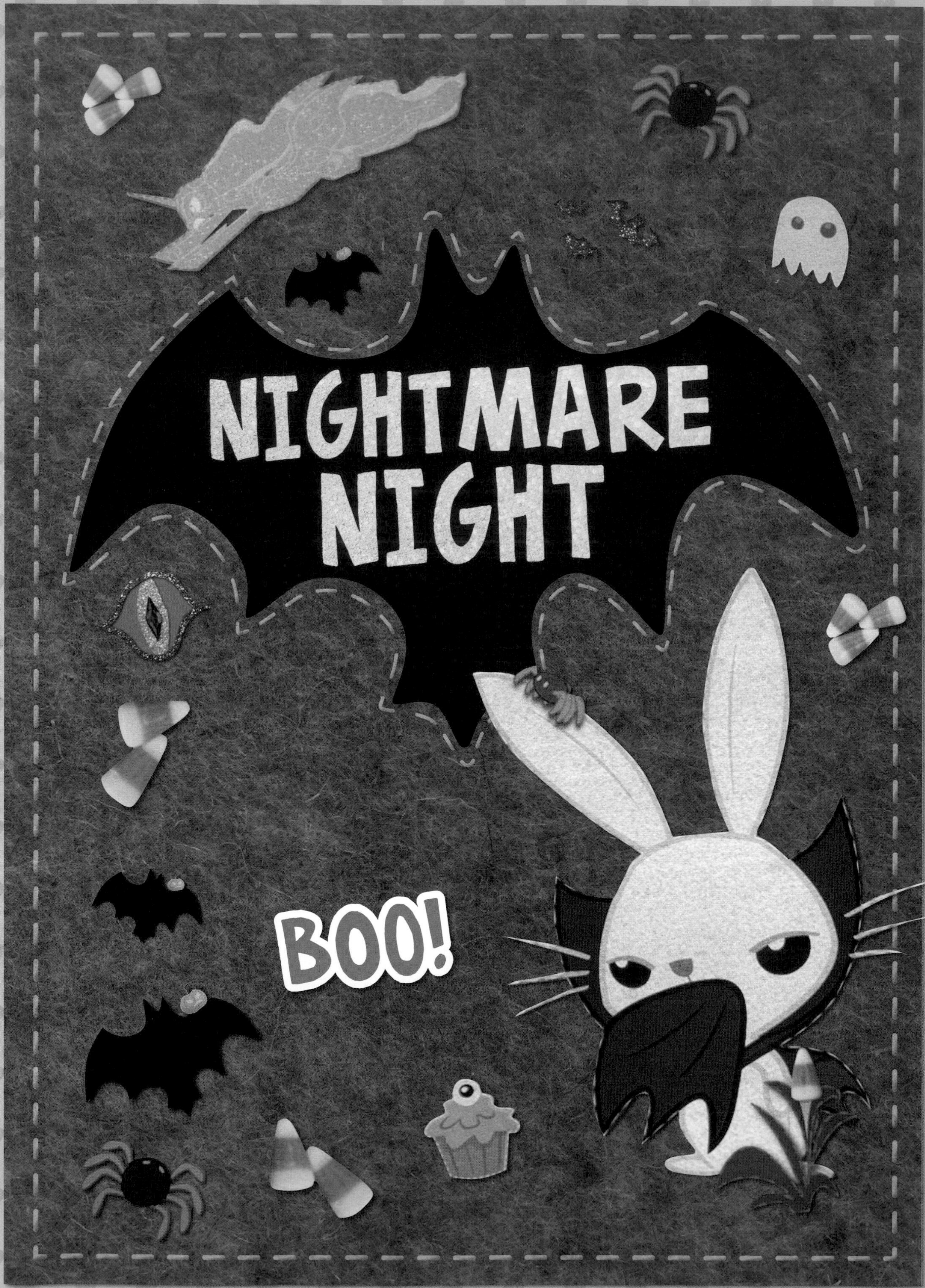
NIGHTMARE NIGHT
BOO!

Every night, when it's time for the ponies to rest their heads, it's up to Princess Luna to use her magic to raise the moon. She is kind and wise, but she wasn't always the sweet, friendly princess everypony knows her to be.

SHE USED TO BE VERY DIFFERENT!

A long time ago, she grew angry that ponies played during the day but slept through the beautiful night that she created for them. Princess Luna was jealous of her sister, Princess Celestia. While Princess Luna rose the moon, Princess Celestia rose the sun. Princess Luna didn't think it was fair that everypony enjoyed the daytime and not her nighttime!

Princess Luna just couldn't take it anymore. Her jealousy overtook her and turned her heart black. Princess Luna was so angry, she transformed herself into **NIGHTMARE MOON.**

109

She wanted to punish everypony by making it **STAY NIGHT FOREVER!** Even her sister, Princess Celestia, wouldn't be able to raise her precious sun. The moon would hang high in the sky—FOREVER!

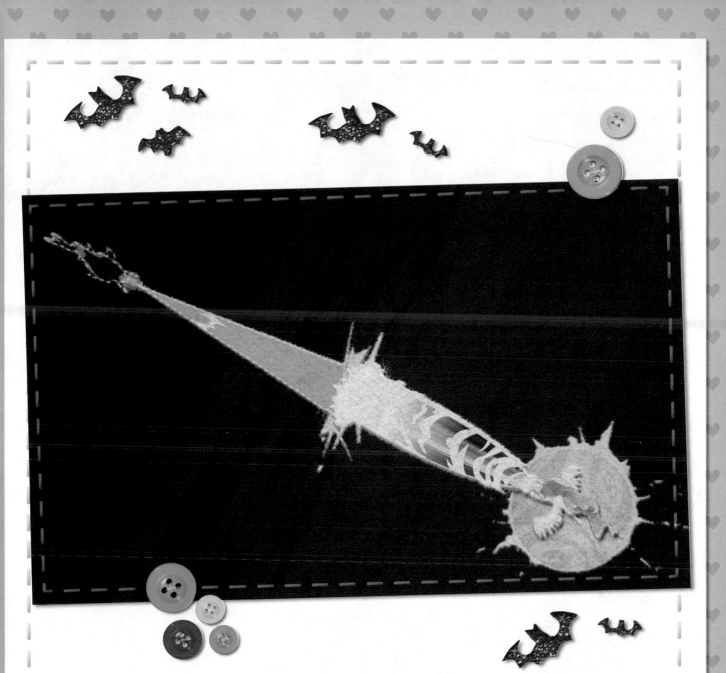

But Princess Celestia wasn't going to give up that easily. She needed to save Equestria and her sister from this never-ending night. Princess Celestia challenged her sister to an epic battle. Using the POWER of their magical horns, they discovered they were equally matched and stayed locked in battle.

The battle proved to be too fierce for the sisters. Celestia was forced to trap her sister in the

MOON for a thousand years!

Soon, the story of Nightmare Moon became something that ponies would tell colts and fillies around campfires and at bedtime to **SCARE THEM.**

Eventually, ponies created a whole holiday to celebrate the story of Nightmare Moon.

THEY CALL IT NIGHTMARE NIGHT.

The ponies decorate every inch of Equestria with spooky things, like ghoulish ornaments and giant pumpkins. Everypony buzzes with excitement when the sun sets on Nightmare Night.

Ponies get to DRESS UP in all kinds of amazing costumes. They go out to parties and play games and eat sweets.

When a pony dresses up, they can be anything they want to be. They can be a dancer, an astronaut, a lion, or even a mermaid!

One time, PINKIE PIE DRESSED UP LIKE A CHICKEN. Lots of ponies thought it was the best costume ever! She even acted like a chicken all night. She pecked at the ground and picked up candy with her mouth!

PINKIE PIE WAS PRETTY PROUD.

Nightmare Night is a night for telling

SPOOKY STORIES

and pulling PRANKS.

Everypony gets really scared but in a fun way! Pranksters like Pinkie Pie and Rainbow Dash have

THE GREATEST TIME.

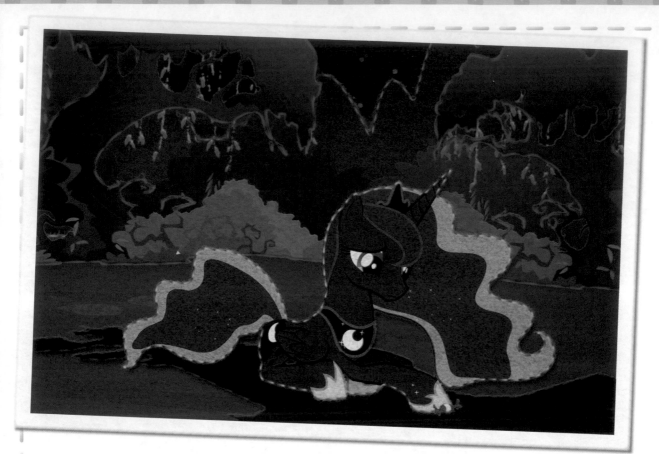

When Princess Luna finally came back from being banished to the moon, she learned about Nightmare Night and GOT VERY SAD.

Her feelings were hurt because there was a whole holiday all about ponies being scared of her.

Twilight Sparkle showed Luna that everypony likes to be a little scared. It's all part of the fun!

Well, everypony
EXCEPT FLUTTERSHY.

Now ponies still ENJOY NIGHTMARE NIGHT. They still dress up in costumes and scare other ponies, but they also celebrate it because Nightmare Moon is gone and they have Princess Luna back. And that is a great thing to celebrate.

Princess Luna and Princess Celestia are the perfect balance. Princess Celestia forgave her sister, and now they raise the sun and moon every day and every night. Together, they keep Equestria harmonious.

HAPPY NIGHTMARE NIGHT, EVERYPONY!

EQUESTRIA

WELCOME TO EQUESTRIA!

It's a magical place full of incredible things to do and areas to explore. There are so many different places with so many different kinds of ponies. So pack up and pull out the map. LET'S GO!

There's the beauty and majesty of **CANTERLOT**. That's where Princess Luna and Celestia live. Princess Luna and Princess Celestia are magical Alicorn sisters. It's their job to raise the sun in the morning and raise the moon at night. Canterlot is also where they hold the **GRAND GALLOPING GALA** every year to **CELEBRATE THE BUILDING OF CANTERLOT.**

There are also the simple charms of PONYVILLE. Some would say that Ponyville is the heart of Equestria.

IT'S CERTAINLY WHERE SOME OF THE COOLEST PONIES LIVE!

That includes Princess Twilight Sparkle, Pinkie Pie, Rainbow Dash, Applejack, Fluttershy, and Rarity!

Right next door to Ponyville, there's the magic and mystery of the **EVERFREE FOREST.**

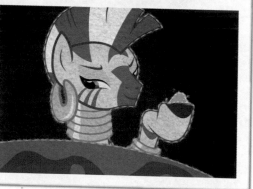

Nopony knows all its secrets— well, except maybe Zecora. She is the mysterious Zebra who lives in the Everfree Forest. She's covered from head to hoof in beautiful stripes and gold jewelry. Her home is in the trunk of an ancient tree. She is always happy to help anypony who comes knocking on her door seeking answers or a healing potion!

If it's hustle and bustle a pony craves, he or she
need look no further than **MANEHATTAN.**

That's where to find
the latest fashions
or catch a show on
Bridleway.

Rough-and-tumble ponies can head on out to **APPLELOOSA,** where the ponies and Buffalo have learned to share the land together. Spend time at the Salt Block saloon, catch a musical performance, or enjoy the acres and acres of apple orchards. The best tour guide in Appleloosa is Braeburn, Applejack's cousin. Braeburn knows everything you need to know about Appleloosa.

Ponies who can fly can head on up to **CLOUDSDALE** to see how the Pegasi make clouds, snow, and rainbows at the weather factory. The whole city is made of clouds.

Speaking of rainbows, there's the swap meet at **RAINBOW FALLS**. Ponies can always find what they're looking for there—like rare books and fun knickknacks!

Lucky ponies may get to go visit the Griffons in their home, GRIFFONSTONE. They should be careful not to sing while there, since it is not allowed!

Or they can go north and see the Yaks in **YAKYAKISTAN.** That's where Prince Rutherford rules. He can be a little short-tempered. One time he visited Ponyville and busted everything up!

There's **LAS PEGASUS**. It's a loud and colorful city in the clouds. They love to have parties there. Ponies like to visit for fun rides, games, stage shows, and amazing food.

Art lovers and foodies love to visit big cities like **BALTIMARE.**

History buffs FLOCK TO FILLYDELPHIA!

They can check out the Liberty Bell. Pinkie Pie didn't crack the bell, she promises!

VANHOOVER has stunning views of mountains and the ocean.

NEIGHAGRA FALLS is a refreshing tourist spot where ponies can take boat rides, swim, or just enjoy the view of one of the biggest waterfalls in Equestria.

There are tons of other great places in Equestria! Whether you are traveling by hoof or by hot air balloon, you are sure to get to where you're going in style. There are always going to be **NEW PLACES TO EXPLORE** for an adventurous pony. And what do new places have? **NEW FRIENDS!**

APPLEWOOD

THE CRYSTALLING

When Flurry Heart was born, the Crystal Empire
had the BIGGEST CRYSTALLING EVER.
Pinkie Pie was one of the first ponies to receive
the beautiful invitation.
It came on a crystal
snowflake and had very
fancy writing. Pinkie
Pie was so excited! She
couldn't wait to celebrate
Flurry Heart at this
amazing Crystalling event.

A **CRYSTALLING** is when all the ponies in the Crystal Empire gather around the **CRYSTAL HEART** and see a **NEW BABY** for the very first time.

The **LOVE** from all the ponies **FLOWS INTO THE HEART,** making it even stronger so it can **PROTECT THE WHOLE EMPIRE.** The Crystal Empire is built on love and the power of the Crystal Heart. A Crystalling fills up the heart, making it super strong. The heart's protection spell keeps all the ponies in the Crystal Empire safe.

But wouldn't you know it, things didn't go quite so smoothly for **FLURRY HEART'S CRYSTALLING.**

When all the ponies showed up, Flurry Heart's dad, Shining Armor, was just so TIRED from taking care of a new baby, he wasn't up for a big party. Shining Armor needed a good night's sleep. But all the ponies from every corner of Equestria had traveled so far for the Crystalling, there was no way they could cancel it.

Princess Cadance wasn't sure what to do.

Flurry Heart could already FLY like a Wonderbolt and use MAGIC like a much older Unicorn. This made sense because Flurry Heart was an extremely powerful and rare pony. She was an Alicorn. That means she had a magical horn like a Unicorn and wings like a Pegasus.

Flurry Heart was the first pony to be born with all the powers of an Alicorn. So as you can imagine, she was quite the hoof-ful for new parents.

Keeping a magical baby pony under control was no easy feat—no wonder why Shining Armor was exhausted! But it wasn't Flurry Heart's fault. Sometimes she couldn't control her powers.

When they took Flurry Heart to the Crystal Heart for her Crystalling, she ACCIDENTALLY used her magic to BLAST the Crystal Heart into a MILLION TINY PIECES!

Everypony knew that THINGS JUST GOT REALLY BAD.

Without the heart, a HUGE STORM BEGAN TO GATHER around the Crystal Empire. The cold and windy dangerous weather of the north THREATENED EVERYPONY in the Empire.

The Crystal Heart had never been broken before. Nopony had ever been powerful enough to break it! That is, until Flurry Heart came along. Now nopony knew what to do.

Princess Cadance was devastated. She assumed all the ponies would just want to go home. But all the Crystal ponies who came to the Crystalling were so excited to meet Flurry Heart that they didn't let the bad weather drive them away.

They wanted to show their

LOVE AND SUPPORT
FOR FLURRY HEART.

The Mane 6 set to work in the library trying to find a spell that could mend the Crystal Heart. There had to be something! Then, Princess Twilight Sparkle found it. A spell book that could help put the crystal pieces back together! Flurry Heart was so excited she . . .

. . . accidentally shot a powerful blast of magic from her horn and destroyed the book. Oops!

A Unicorn named Sunburst figured out just what to do. He knew magic very well, and he had the idea for Starlight Glimmer, Shining Armor, and the princesses to focus their **LOVE AND MAGIC** into repairing the heart.

Sunburst and the Mane 6 gathered Starlight Glimmer, Shining Armor, and the princesses where the Crystal Heart had shattered.

All the ponies silently watched as the powerful ponies focused their magic into the tiny pieces of broken crystal. Little by little, the Crystal Heart became whole, healing itself and saving the Crystal Empire!

Thanks to Sunburst, THE CRYSTAL HEART WAS RESTORED, Flurry Heart's magic calmed down . . .

It was one of the most

AMAZING CRYSTALLINGS

in the history of the Crystal Empire. Through the power of love and magic, the ponies worked together to save the Crystal Empire and restore the protective spell of the Crystal Heart.

Oh, and Flurry Heart had the best time ever! Nopony was ever going to forget this Crystalling.

There are a lot of things colts and fillies may experience as they grow up:

attending a wedding,

foal-sitting little ones,

meeting an Alicorn,

getting a cutie mark,

celebrating Hearth's Warming Eve and Nightmare Night,

exploring Equestria,

but most IMPORTANT . . .

. . . **HAVING FRIENDS!** Princess Twilight Sparkle, Pinkie Pie, Fluttershy, Applejack, Rainbow Dash, and Rarity are **EXPERTS ON FRIENDSHIP.** But that wasn't always the case.

Twilight Sparkle brought them all together and taught them a lot. And they taught her a lot. Then they taught one another a lot!

THAT'S HOW FRIENDSHIP IS SUPPOSED TO WORK.

When a pony trusts her pony friends, that's when the magic begins to happen. If you can believe it,

Twilight Sparkle didn't always trust her pony friends. Through the magic of friendship, she now trusts them to always catch her when she falls!

It's always been easy for Pinkie Pie to make friends. Her wallet is full of photos of the pony friends she has made all over Equestria. Check them out!

Pinkie Pie has been friendly and outgoing all her pony life. When she sets out to make a new friend, she always remembers to be herself. One of the best things about Pinkie Pie is that she always makes her new friends feel like they are #1! When making new friends, here are some things to keep in mind along the way.

First, ponies should **ALWAYS BE KIND** to anypony they meet. No matter how they are treated in return, there is always room for **KINDNESS.** Share your snacks with them. A little bunny can't eat a whole carrot by himself! You can also learn your new friend's favorite snack!

PONIES SHOULD BE GENEROUS. They can let other ponies know they are valued. Rarity is a very generous friend. She gave Spike the handsomest bow tie Equestria had ever seen. It was bright red with gorgeous crystals. Spike loved it. Thank you, Rarity!

They should **ALWAYS BE HONEST.**
Friends help their friends by being honest with them. If you are honest, they are less likely to be grumpy when you've taken a bite out of their cake. Or two bites. Or even THREE bites!

It might be hard sometimes,
but ponies appreciate a friend who
can **TELL THEM HOW IT IS.**

Ponies should **ALWAYS BE LOYAL** to those **PONIES THEY TRUST.**

They can always be there for
them through thick and thin.

Finally, ponies should always remember to laugh. When times get tough, it's good to have a friend who can BRING ON **THE LAUGHS.**

Just ask Princess Twilight Sparkle. A well-timed prank is the perfect way to build the bonds of friendship. Even if the prank is at your expense!

If a pony can do all that, then **THE MAGIC OF HAVING FRIENDS WILL ALWAYS BE THERE** and help them share the joys, pains, and everything in between. With pony friends like these, friendship truly is magic!

The End